KT-439-341

CONTENTS

DINO-MIKE

AND THE
DINOSAUR COVE

WRITTEN & ILLUSTRATED BY FRANCO

Raintree is an imprint of Capstone Global Library Limited, a
company incorporated in England and Wales having its registered
office at 264 Banbury Road, Oxford, OX2 7DY – Registered company
number: 6695582

www.raintree.co.uk
myorders@raintree.co.uk

Edited by Sean Tulien
Designed by Heidi Thompson
Production by Tori Abraham

ISBN 978 1 4747 1004 6
20 19 18 17 16
10 9 8 7 6 5 4 3 2 1

British Library Cataloguing in Publication Data
A full catalogue record for this book is available from
the British Library.

Printed and bound in China.

Young Mike Evans travels the world with his dino-hunting dad and his best friend, Shannon. From the Jurassic Coast in Great Britain to the Liaoning Province in China, young Dino-Mike has been there, *dug* that!

When his dad is dusting fossils, Mike's boning up on his own dino skills — only he's finding the real deal. A live T-rex egg! A portal to the Jurassic Period!! An undersea dinosaur sanctuary!!!

Prepare yourself for another wild and wacky Dino-Mike adventure, which nobody will ever believe...

Chapter 1
WELCOME TO AUSTRALIA

Mike and his dad had arrived in Australia. The plane touched down smoothly and without any problems.

The flight might be the only thing that'll go smoothly on this trip, thought Mike.

Mike's dad, Dr Evans, was a palaeontologist. He was attending a conference of leading palaeontologists. He hoped to find out why the dinosaur bones he'd been digging up in China had disappeared.

The thing is, Mike already knew the answer. Secretly, he and Shannon were on this trip to hunt for Mr Bones. So much had happened that Mike's father had no idea about.

As the plane reached the gate, Mike thought about what had happened in China. Mr Bones, a skeleton-faced bad guy, was stealing Dinosaur skeletons and reanimating them as his own personal slaves. Mike and Shannon had managed to foil his first plan in China, where he brought a complete P-Rex and C. Yangi back to life.

Mike frowned. Despite stopping Mr Bones, they had to leave Ms Li Jing, their Chinese guide, behind. When they had arrived back at Dr Broome's underwater research centre, they told him everything that had happened.

Dr Broome was concerned to say the

least. He even made Mike and Shannon undergo complete physical examinations to make sure they were okay. Then he had Mike's dino hoodie fully checked out – and upgraded.

Beyond that, Dr Broome hadn't been much help. All they knew was Ms Li Jing's driver, Chen, was Mr Bones. They didn't know where he was, or what his next plan would be. Worse still, he was still holding Ms Li Jing hostage.

So, Shannon and Mike came up with a plan to try to locate Mr Bones based on what they knew about him. He would certainly be searching for complete dinosaur skeletons, which narrowed the areas of the world he might be down to two locations – both of them in Australia. That's why Shannon, Mike and Mike's dad were currently pulling up to the gate at terminal #1 in Sydney.

It hadn't taken much effort to convince Dr Evans that Australia would be a good place to look for answers. But as far as Dr Evans knew, Mike and Shannon were just coming along to do some sightseeing.

The three of them made their way to the baggage reclaim. They travelled light, carrying what they could in rucksacks. They did, however, need to pick up one piece of checked baggage.

"Bark! Bark!" came a familiar sound from behind Mike. He turned to watch the airport handlers wheel out a big crate. It jostled side to side as Ahfu, Ms Li Jing's strange dog, bounced around excitedly. The minute Mike unlatched the crate, the panda-like dog tackled him to the ground. Afterwards, he bounced around, stopping occasionally to lick each of their faces.

Mike had suggested Ahfu should come along. He might be able to sniff out Ms Li Jing's location, after all. Shannon quietly pointed out to Mike that Ahfu had a nose for dinosaurs, too. His growls and barks would alert them when one was near.

"I'm off to the hotel," said Mike's father.

Mike narrowed his eyes. He wondered why his dad wasn't more worried about letting him go off and explore Australia with just Shannon. He was usually a lot more protective than that. But Mike wasn't about to bring it up.

Together, the three of them headed

towards the airport's exit. Once out
on the kerb, Mike heard someone call
Shannon's name. He turned to see a big
burly man wearing a straw hat, a crazy
Hawaiian shirt, bright blue shorts and a
bushy moustache.

"Uncle Reno!" shouted Shannon. She ran up to him and gave him a big hug.

Mike smiled. "Security officer Broome," he said. "What are you doing here?"

"Call me Reno, please," the man said. "I only go by my job title when I'm on duty at the museum."

Mike's dad shook hands with Reno. "How are you, Reno?" he asked. "I'm glad you could make it."

"Wouldn't miss it for the world, Dr Evans," Reno said. "I always love coming back to Australia."

Shannon was right, thought Mike. *Reno would be a great guide – he also* knew all about their dinosaur-related secrets. That meant Shannon and Mike wouldn't have to keep quiet around him.

Reno leaned in towards Mike. "I hear you've had quite the adventure since I last saw you, 'Dino-Mike'." he whispered. "Nice work wrangling those dinos that were causing trouble in China, my man."

Mike blushed, but nodded. While he had in fact done those things, Shannon had been just as vital to their success.

Ahfu barked at Mr Reno. "Is this the newest member of our team?" asked Reno. He stooped over to pet the dog. Ahfu barked and jumped up on Uncle Reno, knocking him to the ground.

Shannon giggled. "I think he likes you, Uncle Reno," she said.

"Is it a panda?!" Reno cried.

The dog did in fact look like a panda, which made Shannon giggle even harder. "Nope!" she said. "His fur is just dyed and cut to look like one."

After Ahfu had calmed down, Dr Evans told Mike to be on his best behaviour while he was away – and to listen to Reno. Mike told him he would.

Mike, Shannon and Reno waved goodbye as the cab carried his father away. Then they settled into the 4x4 that Reno had rented.

"It's cool that the museum gave you time off," said Mike.

"Oh, I don't work for the museum," Reno said.

"What?" Mike said. "I thought you were a security guard there."

"I am," replied Reno. "But I work for my brother, Henry. He and the museum have an arrangement so that I can spot anything odd or dinosaur related. Kind of like when you showed up with those eggs a while back."

It all made sense to Mike now. Shannon's dad had people in all the right places to look out for certain things. *That must be how Dr Broome manages to keep the entire world from finding out about living dinosaurs when they pop up, Mike realized.*

It made Mike feel better that an adult was there. Sure, he and Shannon had proven themselves time and time again – but adults tended to make it easier to get places, and they were definitely taken more seriously by others. It'd make their job a lot easier to have him around.

"So this baddie your father was telling me about," Reno said. "What is his deal?"

Shannon sunk in her seat a little bit. "Mr Bones is a mean one, uncle Reno," she said. "He has the ability to reanimate dinosaur skeletons."

One of Reno's thick eyebrows perked up. "Reanimate?" he repeated. "As in ... bring them back to life?"

"Yep!" Shannon said. "And he's got a really mean streak. He even kidnapped our..." She trailed off not wanting to finish that sentence. "I hope Ms Li Jing is all right."

Reno chuckled as he navigated the road. "Not to worry, my dear!" he said. "We'll rescue your old guide. And I guarantee this baddie won't get his boney fingers on me!"

Chapter 2

DINO COVE

Mike got off the phone with his dad, and then sat in silence as Uncle Reno played some tribal music on the 4x4's sound system. Reno spouted off information about Australia as they drove past different landmarks.

Shannon saw that Mike was lost in his own thoughts. "You haven't said much so far, Mike," she said. "Are you sure you're okay?"

Mike sighed. "I know what we're doing is important," he said, "but I don't like keeping secrets from my dad. I mean, your family knows everything you're doing, but I have to keep everything from mine..."

Reno nodded. "I've been in your shoes, my boy," he said. "Back in the day, my brother decided to tell me what he and his wife had kept secret for so long. Knowing what they knew was hard because I had to keep everything from my parents. But honestly, they were probably better off – otherwise they would've been constantly worrying about me and Shannon's dad."

Mike wasn't sure he agreed, but it did help a little to know others had experienced the same thing. "I suppose you're right," he said.

"I know I am!" said Reno. "But don't you fret. We'll get this Mr Bones under control before he does any more damage."

"There's been no sign of him since we last saw him in China," said Shannon.

"We battled with Mr Bones twice on that trip," Mike said. "And had to use the portal key to jump back in time to escape. It was a close call to say the least."

Reno nodded soberly. "I can see why old Henry would be concerned about you children," he said. "However, I'm sure he ran every test he could think of to make sure you two were okay after your ordeal."

Mike nodded. All those tests and needles and scanning machines had hardly seemed worth it – even when they determined that Mike and Shannon were okay. Dr Broome meant well, but all that poking and prodding was more than a little bit annoying.

"Anyway, back to the tour!" said Reno. "We're currently heading towards Victoria. Henry tells me it is a fossil-bearing site..."

Reno's words faded into the background as Mike leaned back in his seat and stared at the scenery flashing past. He snuggled up next to Ahfu, who was asleep next to him. Before he knew it, Mike was asleep too. And he was going to need all the rest he could get.

As he dozed, Mike's thoughts wandered to Australia. It was a beautiful country. Everywhere he looked, there was breathtaking scenery. Back in Atlantis, Dr Broome's dino sanctuary, Jurassic Jeff (Shannon's older brother) warned Mike about Australia.

"Everything there will kill you, Mike!" Jurassic Jeff had said.

Jeff went on to tell them that Australia has something like seven of the world's ten deadliest snakes, salt-water crocodiles, fresh water alligators, hungry sharks, stinging jellyfish, boot-hiding scorpions and just about anything else that could cause pain.

Later, to ease his mind, Mike had looked up the information Jurassic Jeff had spouted off. It turns out he was wrong: Australia had *eight*, not seven, of the ten deadliest snakes. He'd been right about the rest though.

That's when Shannon had pointed out that Mike had been chased by dinosaurs and lived to tell the tale. She was right, of course. He had survived a P-Rex! What was one puny little snake or angry alligator in comparison?

The 4x4 slowed down. Uncle Reno parked up. Mike awoke with a start.

"Come on Mike," Shannon said as she jumped out of the car. Ahfu went bounding out after her. "Don't you want to see Dinosaur Cove?"

"Aw, yeah!" Mike said, scrambling out of the car after her.

Mike had heard about Dino Cove since he was a little boy from his father's stories.

The land ahead looked flat. Nothing he saw looked like a cove at all. But as they got closer, he could hear the sound of water. Soon after, the unmistakable crash of waves.

But he still couldn't see anything. He cranked his neck left and right, trying to spot the source of the sound. That's when he was suddenly pulled back by his hood.

"Whoa there!" Reno said, holding Mike back. "You really need to watch your step around here."

When Uncle Reno let Mike go, he carefully took a few steps closer to the edge. When he looked down, he saw the top of a sheer cliff face. Amazingly, they were several hundred feet above the ocean. If Uncle Reno hadn't stopped him, Mike would've fallen to his death.

"Wow," squeaked Mike, his eyes trained below.

"Exactly," said Uncle Reno. "The first

time I saw this view, that was the same exact word I used."

"Yeah, an awesome view, right?" said Shannon.

Mike agreed, but then started to look around at everything. "Wait, where's the dinosaur dig site?" he asked. "Didn't you say it was here in Victoria?"

Shannon grinned. "You're looking at it," she said.

Mike looked down at the cliff face as the waves crashed against them way down at the bottom. He looked back up at Shannon and raised an eyebrow.

Shannon smiled. "Yep," she said. "You are standing on one of the largest deposits of fossilized dinosaur bones in the world." She looked down over the edge once again. "My father has been in charge of this site for years. He's been developing the safest way to extract the bones without damaging any of the local area. He was planning to put your dad in charge of the entire operation."

"What?" Mike said. "That's got to be an impossible job. How are they supposed to get to the bones?"

"It's not easy, but that's why my dad wanted us to check this site," she said. "If Mr Bones can lift fossils right out of the ground this would be easy for him."

Ahfu started to whine and growl

in a nervous sort of way. Then the ground started to rumble. It was barely noticeable at first, but grew steadily with each passing second.

"Is it an earthquake?" asked Shannon.

"None like I've ever felt!" said Reno.

Between where they stood and where their car was parked, a hole began to open up.

Then, as if using his own private Earth elevator, Mr Bones rose out of the ground.

Chapter 3

MR BONES IS BACK!

Mike couldn't believe his eyes. "Mr Bones!" he cried.

The ground moved like quicksand in a perfect circle about the size of a hula-hoop. As Mr Bones's feet came level with the ground, the sandy earth and rock filled the hole beneath his feet and solidified. Mr Bones floated down so that both his feet were firmly on the ground.

Alifu barked. Mike, Shannon and Reno were all in shock.

Mr Bones spoke, breaking the silence. "What are you doing here?" he growled. His voice sounded like rocks grinding against each other. Though his voice sounded a little different to Mike. He sounded surprised.

Mr Bones wasn't expecting us to be here, Mike realized.

Shannon got straight to the point. "Where is Ms Li Jing?!" she demanded.

Ahfu barked and edged towards Mr Bones. Surprisingly, the villain backed away. To Mike, Mr Bones seemed uncertain – maybe even a little confused.

Mr Bones made an unusual motion with his gloved right hand. The faint rustle of feathers immediately followed. To a casual observer, the rustling wouldn't have meant anything. But Mike knew exactly what was coming.

"Shannon – get down!" he yelled.

The C. Yangi swooped down over Mike and Shannon. They both narrowly avoided being scooped up by the flying dinosaur.

Mike and Shannon knew the winged

dinosaur all too well. The C. Yangi was

a smaller member of the raptor family

of dinosaurs that had feathers over most of its body. It had wings on both its fore and hind legs. Though no larger than a turkey, it had razor-sharp talons and teeth designed for shredding flesh.

Even worse, the C. Yangi was under the complete control of Mr Bones, like some sort of prehistoric, flying attack dog!

Ahfu started barking furiously at the feathered dinosaur. The barking caused the C. Yangi to hesitate. Uncle Reno immediately sprang into action – and dove onto the C.Yangi's back!

The C. Yangi twisted and turned, but Reno's dino-wrangling skills were on full display. He had the C. Yangi in a headlock before anyone knew what was happening. Mr Bones made furious hand gestures to send signals to the C. Yangi, but the dinosaur could only watch and not act.

Mike was ready and waiting for the distinct, audible pop that accompanied an attack by Mr Bones. Every time it happened, it meant Mr Bones was transporting a new dinosaur to the scene.

But to Mike's surprise, Mr Bones just stood there with slumped shoulders.

"You don't have more dino slaves to summon, do you?" said Mike. "The C. Yangi is all you have left now that we took your Pinocchiosaurus!"

Mr Bones growled. "You kids have caused nothing but trouble for us!"

"That's because you're doing things that you shouldn't be!" said Shannon.

"Us?" said Mike.

"What about your father?" Mr Bones asked Shannon. "Has he not upset the balance of things already with his deeds?"

"My father?" asked Shannon. "What are you talking about?"

"Do not play coy with me," said Mr Bones. "Where have you taken my Pinocchiosaurus Rex? Or, perhaps, 'when' have you taken him?"

Before Shannon could respond, there was a rush of air and a loud *POP!* Just like that, Mr Bones was gone.

Shannon pumped her fist. "The C. Yangi must have been his only dino slave!" she said. "It means he's having problems finding intact whole dinosaur skeletons to reanimate."

Mike nodded. "We're lucky we beat him here, then," he said.

"Lucky indeed!" said Reno, still struggling to hold the C. Yangi down. "I don't want to think what this guy would've done with an army of dinosaurs."

Uncle Reno was struggling to control the C. Yangi. "Mike, could you kindly fetch the containment device from the back of my 4x4?" he asked.

"On it!" Mike said.

Reno positioned the C. Yangi so they could use the containment field to trap it.

Mike held up the device. "So if Mr Bones has gone, that probably means he hasn't found any intact skeletons here, right?" he asked.

"Seems so," Reno said with a nod.

A sudden rush of air was followed by a loud *POP!* Smoke filled the immediate area. Unlike earlier, Mr Bones's entrance was particularly dramatic.

"I think I spoke too soon," Reno said.

Chapter 4
STAMPEDE

Oddly, Mike thought Mr Bones looked bigger than he had a few minutes ago. Coupled with the dramatic entrance, Mike had to admit he was feeling a bit intimidated.

Ahfu, on the other hand, wasn't fazed. He growled and barked at Mr Bones with even more enthusiasm than before.

"Now's our chance!" said Shannon. "Uncle Reno, Mike – get that feathered thing into a containment box. Then we can take Mr Bones down once and for all!"

Mr Bones gestured with his hand. "You think that is my only dinosaur?" he growled. "My dear, you are sorely mistaken!"

The ground beneath their feet started to rumble and shift. It didn't feel like an earthquake. More like sand or loose soil shifting underfoot. The ground started to change shape. Little patches of dirt shifted all around Mike, as if a pile of sand was sifting through a giant's fingers.

Mike felt panic rising in his chest. "Uh-oh," he said.

"He's bringing a dinosaur back to life!" cried Shannon. "And it sounds like a big one!"

Mr Bones laughed in his gravelly voice. He continued his hand gestures. "Not just *a* dinosaur ... *lots of them!*"

A dino emerged from the shifting sands. It wasn't all that big, but neither was the next one that appeared. Or the next one – or the one after that.

In a matter of moments, dozens of little dinos had surrounded Mike, Shannon and Reno. Each one was no larger than a chicken, but more of them were popping up every second.

Reno was still holding back the C. Yangi. His eyes were wide and his mouth was open, but he wasn't speaking.

"Don't worry," said Shannon. "They are small theropods."

Uncle Reno looked slightly relieved. That is, until Mike said, "Aren't theropods ... carnivorous?"

"They haven't attacked us yet," Shannon said uncertainly. "And Ahfu isn't even barking at them. They look like the Skartopus, which eats insects, frogs, and reptiles."

"Impressive!" Mr Bones said. "You certainly know your dinosaurs ... but how well do you know dinosaur history?"

Once again, Mr Bones moved his hand in a strange gesture.

"History?" asked Shannon. "What are you talking about?"

"Did something dino-related happen here?" asked Mike.

"Stampede..." Reno said between his teeth.

Mr Bones just laughed.

"Stampede? What do you mean, Uncle Reno?" asked Shannon.

Reno stared at the chicken sized dinosaurs. There were about fifty or sixty – maybe even a hundred. And they kept coming.

"There was a quarry," Reno said,

straining against the C. Yangi. "A lake
bed with hundreds of small dinosaur
tracks."

"So what?" said Mike. "What harm
could these little dinos do to us?"

Shannon's eyes went wide. "Not
them!" she realized. "It's what was
making them stampede!"

Ahfu started to growl low. Sure enough, the earth started to shake again – but this time it did feel like an earthquake. A large open area of ground about ten metres away from them started to sift and move.

A huge beast lifted itself up from the

ground. It seemed to Mike to be almost six metres long. Its neck was short and it had an elongated head. A small pair of horns poked out above its eyes, and ridges ran along the bridge of its nose. The head and neck of this beast led down to a massive body held up by two very powerful hind limbs and a large tail.

The first thing it did was snort and huff, clearing any sand or dirt that had collected on its face. Mike gulped when he saw that the dino's open mouth contained a lot of serrated teeth.

"Allosaurus!" hissed Reno.

"Oh, boy," said Mike. "When that thing notices the little fellas –"

The roar of the Allosaurus shattered the air and the hundred or so tiny dinosaurs started running. At first it reminded Mike of a school of fish at the aquarium, moving like one big body.

And they were heading right towards him!

Reno was forced to give up his hold on the C. Yangi.

Shannon started to run away from the stampede. They had all been in situations where they had to think on their feet and move when there was a threat of a dinosaur attack.

What they didn't count on was dealing with a panda-like dog rising up and barking at the oncoming herd.

"Mike!" Shannon yelled as he ran towards Ahfu. "Help!"

Mike sprinted. As he neared Ahfu, he slid down to his knees and scooped him up in his arms. By that point, the stampede was already upon them. Mike stuffed Ahfu inside his jacket, zipped it up tight, and turned away from the terrified, tiny dinos.

Mike could feel the pitter-pat of tiny feet all around him – and over him! Thankfully the tough dino-like scales that Dr Broome had lined the outside of the jacket with were living up to the hype. The tiny dinos' sharp little claws barely tickled as dozens of dino feet ran over him.

And then it was over. Mike stood up and began to run – only to find the Allosaurus staring at him less than a metre away from his nose.

Chapter 5

ALLOSAURUS ATTACK!

The Allosaurus had clearly never seen a human before. The beast's head was tilted and Mike could feel and hear (and smell) the Allosaurus's breath through its nostrils.

It took a couple more deep inhalations. Then Mike noticed that the muscles on the Allosaurus's neck began to flex and tighten. He knew what that meant: the dinosaur was about to let loose a deafening roar, then probably eat him (along with Ahfu). He was about to get a roar in his face and a good look at the inside of that toothy mouth. The roar would probably be followed by the dinosaur trying to eat him. He wanted to avoid both of those things.

Mike quickly reached up and pulled on his hood. His recent experiences with dinosaurs had taught him that the element of surprise was usually a good way to avoid being eaten.

The two eyes on the sides of Mike's hood looked like a T-rex's for a reason: they sent even the most fierce dinosaurs back a step or two, at the least. But the best part of the hoodie was its T-rex roar!

As the speakers in Mike's hoodie issued forth a massive dino-growl, the Allosaurus's eyes went as wide as they could. Instead of letting out its own roar, now it was suddenly scrambling away from Mike as fast as it could.

As the Allosaurus did what Mike had come to call the "dino shuffle", he sprinted off in the opposite direction.

"I can't believe you did that!"
Shannon cried, running next to Mike.

"I had to! Ahfu was in trouble!"
he said. "I couldn't just leave him out
there."

Shannon smiled warmly. She was
about to say something when a muffled
bark came from inside Mike's dino
hoodie. Then Ahfu's head poked out, his
tongue wagging happily.

Once Reno caught up with them,
they stopped to catch their breath.
"What do we do now?" Mike asked.

They turned back to see that smoke
was billowing around the area again. Mr
Bones was gesturing, which meant the

C. Yangi or the Allosaurus – or both – would be coming at them soon.

"No one move!" boomed Mr Bones.

"We can't outrun either dinosaur," Shannon pointed out. "And there's nowhere to hide…"

Mike looked up and to the left for a moment. Then he pulled one of Shannon's dinosaur containment traps out from his pocket. "If we can get close enough to Mr Bones," Mike said, "we could trap him in one of these."

"It's worth a shot!" said Uncle Reno.

"Agreed," said Shannon.

"Turn around and face me!" commanded Mr Bones.

Mike slipped the containment trap back into his pocket. Before he turned to face Mr Bones, he made sure that Ahfu was once again concealed inside his hoodie.

Mr Bones stood tall, flanked by C. Yangi on one side and the recovered Allosaurus on the left. There was no question that they were both under his control. Both dinosaurs were clearly waiting for his next command.

Mike knew how Mr Bones was able to command the dinosaurs. Well, sort of ... Dr Broome had explained to him that Mr Bones was probably using tiny little robots, called nano-bots, to control the dinosaurs, which had probably been injected into them.

Mike had then pointed out that Mr Bones seemed to be controlling the dinosaurs with his gloved hand. Dr Broome then came to the conclusion that Mr Bones was sending orders to the nano-bots by way of subharmonics – a sort of radio signal.

That was the part Mike was still unclear about. Dr Broome had said that when Mr Bones waved his hand, a song was played that only the dinosaurs could hear. That song caused the nano-bots to force them to follow his commands.

Mike had then asked why they

couldn't just turn the song off or block the signal. Dr Broome explained that unlike normal sound waves, the technology Mr Bones used was able to go through buildings, the ground – even the containment traps.

The only way to turn it off was to get that glove off of Mr Bones's hand. Dr Broome said that would prove to be difficult.

Difficult, thought Mike, *but not impossible.*

"I want only Mike to step forward," growled Mr Bones.

Shannon narrowed her eyes. "Why?"

"You know why!" Mr Bones said. "I want that jacket — and I will not tolerate interference this time, young lady."

Mike knew he had to play along. He stepped forward and unzipped his jacket so at least Ahfu would be out of harm's way. To Mike's surprise, Ahfu scrambled out and ran towards Mr Bones – then jumped on him and barked ferociously!

While Mr Bones was struggling with Ahfu on the ground, the dinosaurs were completely still because they hadn't received any instructions from Mr

Bones. Mike took full advantage of the accidental distraction and pulled the dino trap out of his pocket.

With a confident throw, Mike slid the trap along the ground. It came to rest directly beneath Mr Bones. He whistled at Ahfu and the dog came back to him at full speed.

Once Ahfu was clear, Mike immediately activated the switch. A familiar blue cube appeared around Mr Bones, trapping him. "Got him!" yelled Mike.

"Yes!" cried Shannon and Reno.

As they all knew that Mr Bones would still be able to control the dinosaurs from inside the cube, that was the extent of their celebration. Mike produced two more traps, and Shannon and Reno grabbed them and edged towards the dinosaurs.

Please work! thought Mike.

But before Shannon and Reno could activate the traps, the unmistakable sound of racing wind filled the air.

Then came a *POP!*

Mike sighed. I'm really starting to hate that sound, he thought.

"Wait a sec," Mike said. "How can Mr Bones teleport if he's trapped inside the containment field?"

Before anyone could answer, a figure appeared next to the containment field. Mike was sure he was seeing things until Shannon said, "Wait ... there's two of them?!"

One was trapped in the blue containment field. The other was standing next to the containment field.

Mike was staring at twin villains!

Chapter 6

DOUBLE TROUBLE

Both versions of Mr Bones spoke as one. "We want one thing," they echoed. "Your dino hoodie!"

Mike squinted. He could tell there was a height difference between the two villains. Otherwise they looked exactly the same.

"You never mentioned two of them!" said Reno.

"There was only one last time!" said Shannon. "Ms Li Jing's driver!"

Ever since Mike had begun dealing with living dinosaurs, he'd become more and more proactive than reactive. Dr Broome, Shannon and even Jeff had told him it was a good trait to have. Dino dealings tended to be unpredictable and nearly impossible to prepare for – like, for example, the fact there were two versions of Mr Bones!

Mike didn't hesitate – he ran up to the new Mr Bones at full speed. Just before reaching him, Mike activated the balloon mode in his jacket and rammed into Mr Bones number two.

BOING! Mike bounced this Mr Bones off of his feet and sent him flying back about two metres. Mike deflated quickly, looking to press his advantage. He ran up and reached for the villain's gloves before Mr Bones could use them to command the dinosaurs.

Unfortunately, Ahfu thought Mike was playing around – and jumped up on Mike. Ahfu's front paw struck a hidden switch in Mike's hoodie.

CLANK! Stegosaurus plates popped out of the back of the hoodie. Mike pulled Ahfu off him. The playful dog then scurried over to Mr Bones, tail wagging, and jumped up on him.

Mikes eyes went wide. "Wait a minute!" he cried out. "Ahfu knows who you are!"

As Mr Bones shrugged off Ahfu, Mike ran up and pulled off the villain's mask.

Mike's jaw dropped. This Mr Bones wasn't a Mr after all...

"Ms Li Jing!?" Mike cried.

Chapter 7
IDENTITY CRISIS

"I thought Mr Bones was Ms Li Jing's driver, Chen?" asked Reno.

"He is," Mike said, narrowing his eyes. "One of them, anyway."

"So that's how they were able to be in so many places so quickly!" Shannon said.

"Wait," Mike said to Ms Li Jing. "Is Chen making you do this?"

Ms Li Jing laughed. "My brother did not force me to do anything!"

"*Brother*?" asked Mike.

Ms Li Jing stepped face to face with Mike. "In fact," she said proudly, "gathering and reanimating these dinosaurs was my idea, not Chen's! He's just better at controlling them!"

"And we are going to see our plan through ... to the end!" Ms Li Jing said. With surprising speed, she grabbed Mike by the shoulders and pushed him towards the containment cube holding Chen.

"Mike!" Shannon yelled. "Look out!"

The Stegosaurus plates extending

from the back Mike's jacket penetrated
the stasis field of the blue cube. *ZRRRT!*
The electronic parts of the Stegosaurus
plates sparked out arcs of blue energy.

The strange, blue energy surrounded Mike's hoodie and Ms Li Jings gloves. Both the C. Yangi and the Allosaurus flinched at the same time.

BOOM! POOF! The containment field shorted out, causing the walls to vanish.

The other Mr Bones was free!

As Mike fell on his back, the Stegosaurus plates on his hoodie retracted. The edges of his vision grew dark, and he feared he was going to pass out. Reno and Shannon ran towards him, calling out his name.

Before they could reach him, Chen reached down and picked up Mike by his hoodie. At the same time, Ms Li Jing stepped between Mike and his friends. "Do not come any closer!" she warned them. "Or you'll regret it!"

"Don't hurt him!" Shannon cried.

"He will not be harmed as long as you do what we say," Chen growled.

Shannon froze. "Why are you doing this?" she asked.

"You have no one to blame but yourselves," Chen growled. "In China, you two kids ruined our plan to get control of the P-Rex – and refused to give us the the dino hoodie!"

"You'll pay for this," Mike said weakly.

Chen shook him violently. "Quiet!" he growled.

"Hey, leave him alone!" Uncle Reno yelled. "He's just a child. Why don't you try picking on someone your own size?"

Chen held Mike's hoodie more tightly. "This 'child' has been nothing but a big pain ever since I met him!" Chen growled.

Mike smiled, knowing he'd helped to foil their plans – and that Uncle Reno was standing up for him.

Ms Li Jing unzipped Mike's dino hoodie. "You should have just given us this jacket in China like we wanted," she said.

Mike panicked. If they had his jacket, they wouldn't need to find dinosaur skeletons – they'd just go back in time and enslave living ones! No matter what, Mike couldn't let them get their claws on the portal key...

Mike struggled to keep her from taking the jacket. But with Chen holding his arms, he couldn't resist for long. Ahfu, thniking they were playing games, got in on the action by grabbing the jacket's sleeve and pulling.

Chen released Mike to engage in a brief tug of war with Ahfu. Too tired to fight back, Mike collapsed to his knees. Soon, Chen gained possession of the jacket.

Shannon ran over to Mike and hugged him protectively. They all turned

their attention back to the sibling villains. Ms Li Jing held up the jacket as Chen examined it. "Now we will have an army of mighty dinosaurs to do our bidding!" he bellowed. "Nothing can stop us now!"

Mike looked up at Shannon and Uncle Reno. "I'm so sorry..." was all he could manage to say.

Chapter 8

TROUBLE DOG

Chen looked at Ms Li Jing. "Well, sister?" he growled. "Want to see *when* this jacket can take us?"

His sister nodded. "And let's take the boy with us," she said. "He can be our tour guide – and our hostage. That way, these other two troublemakers won't try to stop us."

Mike could see that Reno and Shannon wanted to leap in and help him, but he motioned for them to stay back. The last thing Mike wanted was for Chen to make the Allosaurus angry.

Chen opened the jacket and inspected it. All of the buttons were easy to access, which was by design. The portal key, however, was carefully hidden within the lining of the jacket's right sleeve.

I hope it takes him a while to find it, Mike thought. *It'd buy us some time to –* "When you disappeared in China," Chen said, interrupting Mike's thoughts, "I saw you put your hand in here." He pointed inside the right sleeve.

Mike's head and shoulders sank.

"Cheer up, kid," Chen said. "You get

to go back in time to show us where to find the biggest, baddest dinosaurs."

Mike's head began to spin. Chen was about to transport them all to the past so he could assemble an evil army of killer dinos ... and there was nothing he could do about it.

Suddenly, the jacket was snatched from Chen's hands.

"Hey!" cried Chen. "Bad dog! Bad!"

Ahfu ran off with Mike's jacket between his teeth, thrashing it back and forth like a stuffed dog toy. The site of a panda-like dog running around with a green scaled jacket made Mike laugh.

"I told you to stop yelling at my dog!" Ms Li Jing said to Chen. "I do not like it when you do that!"

"But it's true!" Chen growled. "He's a *very* bad dog!"

While Mr and Ms Bones were arguing, Mike chased after Ahfu. As usual, the dog was in a playful mood and decided to run away from Mike – and everyone else.

Mike and Shannon and Uncle Reno and both of the Bone siblings all chased after the panda-like dog. It looked like a scene from an old comedy film. The only spectators were two confused dinosaurs watching them run back and forth like headless chickens. Mike would've thought the situation hilarious if he weren't entirely focused on getting his jacket back.

"Enough!" Chen growled.

Mr Bones began to make hand gestures. A moment later, the mighty roar of the Allosaurus thundered through the air!

Chapter 9
SHOWDOWN!

The roar made Ahfu drop the jacket – but not because of fear. Mike had come to learn that Ahfu, although friendly, wasn't the type to back down from a big challenge.

And challenges didn't come any bigger than an angry Allosaurus.

Mike knew the little pooch didn't have a chance against the huge dino. Mike raced towards the jacket, scooped it up, and pulled it on as he ran.

Shannon's voice called from behind Mike. However, instead of scolding him, she was cheering him on!

Mike smiled. *That's why she's my best friend,* he thought. *Dino-Mike and Triceratops Shannon: best friends for –*

"That's it!" Mike said to himself. "*Triceratops!*"

Mike reached back to pull his hoodie over his head. He kept two fingers pressed on the hood's right eye, which activated Triceratops Mode.

After his encounter with a real triceratops, Shannon's father had made the upgrade, and Mike was glad of it. Few dinos could stand up to an

Allosaurus, but the Triceratops was one of them.

KIRRRRSH! The back of Mike's jacket rose up. Two more horns emerged from both sides of the hood. The scales on the jacket expanded to triple their normal size.

They now covered Mike's face and hands, and made him look bigger. The jacket even let out the snort of a charging Triceratops!

Still running during the transformation, Mike was able to get between Ahfu and the Allosaurus in the nick of time.

BAM!!! Mike collided with the Allosaurus! The bigger dino put all its weight into Mike, but he didn't move even a centimetre. The scale plates at the bottom of his jacket had embedded

spikes into the ground, much like the body of a real Triceratops would do with its tree-like legs and its low centre of gravity.

If a Triceratops doesn't want to move, Mike thought with a grin, *then he isn't going to move.*

Mike knew it was now or never. With Ahfu running between his legs, Mike concentrated on his task. He reached into the sleeve of his jacket and pulled out the portal gem, a new addition to his dino repertoire that Dr Broome had created after the trip to China.

It was exactly like the portal key Mr and Ms Bones were trying to get their greedy hands on, except it was smaller and therefore more portable. It was attached to a rope with a thickness similar to a fishing line – but much, much stronger.

Mike took out a piece of chewing gum, quickly chewed it a few times, and then stuck it to one end of the gem. While he and the Allosaurus were still locked in a shoving match (that neither of them was winning), Mike reached his hand out between the oversized scales on his jacket.

CLINK! Mike stuck the gem to the belly of the Allosaurus. Then Mike clicked a button inside his jacket to release the plates embedded in the ground and immediately sidestepped out of the way.

The Allosaurus stumbled forwards and nearly fell on its face, but managed to regain its balance at the last second.

Mike didn't hesitate. *CLICK!* He activated the portal gem.

The Allosaurus froze in place as the air around the dinosaur crackled and hummed with invisible energy. Mike quickly retracted the rest of the scales on his jacket, returning him to normal size.

Quickly, Mike pulled on the line, retracting the portal gem off of the Allosaurus's belly just as the giant dinosaur disappeared.

I did it! Mike thought, pumping his fist. He had sent the Allosaurus back

to a time where he could be himself –

a normal dinosaur – and not get any

humans in trouble for it.

More importantly, it meant that

Mr and Ms Bones no longer had their

dinosaur slave!

Mike disabled Triceratops Mode completely. Ahfu tilted his head and looked up at Mike, clearly confused by the whole ordeal. But a moment later, the happy-go-lucky dog was dancing around him again.

Mike patted the dog gently on the head. "Thanks for helping out, Ahfu," he said.

But this was no time for celebration. Mr Bones ran at Mike and pushed him down to the ground. Ahfu began barking furiously at Chen.

"That's the last time you ruin any of my plans!" Mr Bones said in his gravelly voice. The skeleton-masked villain turned towards Ahfu. "Quieten down,

you flea bag!" Then he turned back to
Mike. "You give me that jacket right
now, you little brat! Otherwise I'll make
sure your friends truly suffer – and your
little dog, too!"

SMACK! Before Mike could respond

or even think about responding, Chen was in a heap on the ground right next to him.

Uncle Reno dusted off his hands. "You aren't so tough without your big mean Allosaurus around, are you?" he said in his commanding voice. "I told you before: try picking on someone your own size!"

He sure knocked Chen down to size! thought Mike. He smiled up at Uncle Reno, wondering if the man had played rugby at some point in his life.

Chen rolled to his back and angrily pulled off his mask. "You want to fight someone your own size?" he growled.

"Then it is time you met my not-so-little friend!"

Chen gestured wildly with his gloved hand. Mike's fears were immediately confirmed by the unmistakable sound of the C. Yangi's flapping wings.

Uncle Reno turned his head just in time to see the fine, feathered dinosaur diving down at him with its sharp talons fully extended. There was no time to move, so Reno covered his head with his hands and ducked down.

Mike closed his eyes, afraid to watch.

A moment passed. Then another. No shrieks or screams came. When Mike finally opened his eyes, he saw the dinosaur had somehow been frozen in mid-air less than a metre from Uncle Reno's head.

"What–" Mike stuttered. "How...?"

Then Mike saw the thin, blue walls surrounding the C. Yangi's body. He turned his head to see Shannon smiling wide – and holding a controller for one of the dino traps!

Mike extended his fist into the air. "Way to go, Shan!" he cried.

Shannon smirked at Chen. "You may think you're super-clever and scary," she said, her hands on her hips. "But you're nothing but a dino-bully."

Mike laughed and jumped to his feet. Ahfu crouched and growled at Chen who was still lying on the ground. Reno just silently shook his head at the fallen super-villain.

"You're evil dino-adventures are at an end, Chen," Mike said.

Reno chuckled. "Yep. Mr Bones will be behind bars in no time," he said.

To Mike's surprise, Chen was smiling up at them. "You think so?" he growled.

Mike heard scratching and clicking coming from behind him. Mike wondered what it could be – until he realized he'd forgotten all about the *other* Mr Bones, Ms Li Jing!

Mike turned around. Sure enough, she was gesturing with her glove. The sound Mike had heard was lots of Skartopus stampeding towards him!

"My brother and I are a team," she said. "I may not be as good at commanding dinosaurs as he is, but trampling you with these dinosaurs will be a piece of cake!"

While harmless looking, the only reason they didn't hurt Mike during the last stampede was because of his jacket's armoured scales. Shannon and Uncle Reno didn't have those to keep them safe. If Mike didn't act quickly, they'd be seriously hurt – or even killed.

Mike didn't know what to do! Fortunately, he didn't have to do anything. During the last stampede, Mike had jumped in the way and saved Ahfu. This time, Ahfu stepped up to protect Mike and the others!

The strange dog jumped right in front of the dinosaurs and barked and growled his little heart out. Sure enough, the Skartopus stopped in their tracks.

Mike tilted his head. "Why are they scared of Ahfu?" he said to himself. "He's not much bigger than they are!"

Then Mike realized that Ms Bones had stopped making hand gestures with her glove. She'd been the one who stopped the stampede!

Mike frowned at Ms Li Jing. "Why?" he asked. "Why did you call off your attack?"

Ms Bones lowered her head. "I am sorry, Chen," she said. "I can't hurt Ahfu. He is my dog."

Chapter 10

RUN FOR YOUR LIVES!

As quickly as they'd appeared, the Sharktopus dispersed. Mike smiled down at Ahfu. The dog seemed quite pleased with himself. Mike couldn't blame him.

"Without any dinosaurs to back you up, you don't stand a chance against us," Mike said to Ms Li Jing.

Uncle Reno stopped Chen from getting to his feet by carefully holding the man's arm behind his back. "Say uncle!" he said. "Uncle Reno, that is!"

Chen still wore a smirk on his face. "We knew the chance of finding complete dinosaur bones here was very slim," he said. "But that's not why we came here ... is it sister?"

Ms Bones nodded. "It looks like plan 'B' has begun," she said, glaring angrily at Ahfu. "The opal."

Mike narrowed his eyes. "Opal?" he asked.

"Oh!" said Shannon. "That explains it! That's why they haven't reanimated any other dinosaurs here! Because they can't – they're all opal!"

"What does that mean?" asked Mike. "What's opal?"

"It's a crazy thing that happens only in Australia!" explained Shannon. "They are one of the most beautiful things on the planet. Opal is formed, over long periods of time, when silicon dioxide and water mix together."

"Huh?" Mike grunted.

Shannon continued, "As water runs down through the earth, it picks up silica. You may have heard of it's other name: quartz."

Mike nodded reluctantly. He'd heard of quartz, but was still more than a little bit confused.

"It comes from sandstone," Shannon said. "It's carried into cracks or pockets caused by natural faults or decomposing fossils ... like all the dinosaur bones beneath our feet!"

Mike stared blankly at Shannon. It seemed the more she said, the more confused he became.

Shannon let out an exasperated sigh. "As the water evaporates, it leaves behind a silica deposit. This cycle repeats over very long periods of time to eventually form opals."

"Okay, so there are lots of crystals below us," Mike said. "What does that have to do with these two?" He pointed his thumb towards Mr and Ms Bones.

Mike's eyes went wide in terror. "Are

you trying to say they can bring crystal dinosaurs to life?" he asked.

Shannon rolled her eyes. "No, silly," she said. "But they can pull them out of the ground and sell them for millions of pounds!"

Reno shrugged. "No big deal," he said. "We've got these siblings in our control now. And there are no more dinosaurs to protect them."

Ms Bones made one quick gesture with her gloved hand. At that moment, the ground started to shake.

Suddenly the most beautiful dinosaur bones Mike had ever seen began rising up from the ground.

Ms Bones raised both her gloved

hands into the air. All the opal dinosaur

bones were emerging from the ground and floating in the air!

It was the prettiest, coolest and strangest thing Mike had ever seen.

"You may have won this time, Dino-Mike," Ms Li Jing said. "But next time we meet, the story will end differently!"

"Ahfu! Come!" said Ms Li Jing. Ahfu didn't move.

She waited a few seconds. "Ahfu, come!" she repeated. When she realized he wasn't going to, she sighed. "I see he is no longer *my* pet."

Mike heard the familiar rush of wind. The villain siblings were leaving, and there was nothing he could do about it.

POP! Suddenly Mr and Ms Bones – along with all the opal dinosaur bones – were gone. A fine mist of grey-white powder sparkled in the air around them.

Shannon held out her hand catching some of the powder in her palm as it floated down. She sighed. "Well, they escaped again," she said. "And we still have no idea what this powder is."

BEEP-BEEP!

"Now what?" said Uncle Reno. He glanced around nervously. "Robot dinosaurs?!"

Mike laughed.

"It's good to know you're ready for anything, Reno," Mike said. "But you can relax – it's just my ringtone."

"Oh," Reno said, relaxing.

Mike activated his speaker phone. "Hey, dad," he said.

"Hey Mike! Are you having a good time sightseeing?"

Mike grinned. "I suppose you could say I've seen some pretty interesting things today."

"That's great. So I think I've got a lead on who stole my dinosaur bones in China," Dr Evans said. "It turns out that Ms Li Jing was probably behind the caper with the help of her brother, the chauffeur. They have some crazy idea that they can bring dinosaurs back to life. If you encounter these two, I want you to stay as far away from them as possible. They're likely to be completely crazy."

Mike could barely hold in his laughter. "No worries, dad. I don't think they'll show up in Australia."

"Their father, Dr Jiang," Dr Evans said, "is the world's foremost expert on dino DNA. He was working on a nano-bot technology that would help him find bones buried deep underground and extract them without using heavy machinery."

Mike was already tired of acting surprised. "Wow," he said flatly.

"I know, right?" Dr Evans said. "Anyway, I also heard from Shannon's dad. He said to say the tests he did on the strange powder you two found at the dig site in China came back inconclusive."

"Then what do we do now?" asked Mike.

"Better get back to the hotel," his dad said. "It's time to pack our bags, because we're heading out again soon. I'll tell you where we're going when you get here!"

The call ended. "Where in the world are we going now?" Mike mumbled.

Shannon smiled. "If they're looking

for complete sets of bones, there's only one place left for them to search."

Mike raised an eyebrow. "And where would that be?" he asked.

Shannon grinned and jumped up and down excitedly. "We're going to ANTARCTICA!"

GLOSSARY

Changyuraptor Yangi four-winged predatory dinosaur, also known as C. Yangi

fossil remains, impression or trace of a living thing of a former geologic age, such as a dinosaur bone

Jurassic Period period of time about 200 to 144 million years ago

palaeontologist scientist who studies fossils and other life-forms

Triceratops large, plant-eating dinosaur with three horns and a fan-shaped collar that is made of bone

Tyrannosaurus rex large, meat-eating dinosaur that walked on its hind legs, also known as a T-rex

DINO FACTS!

Theropoda is a species of dinosaur. The word is Greek for "beast feet", which is fitting considering they were quite beastly and quick!

The Theropoda species of dinosaur, or Theropods, first appeared 231.4 million years ago during the Triassic period. Over time, they evolved to become a variety of dinosaur species including the Allosaurus and the Tyrannosaurus Rex, both of which appear in this book.

Theropods include herbivores, carnivores and omnivores. That means the different species ate plants, meat or both. Each different type of Theropod evolved, adapting to their environment, to survive in the most efficient way possible.

How do we know so much about dinosaurs despite the fact that they all became extinct centuries ago? The answer is fossils!

In Latin, the word "fossils" means "obtained by digging". That is because most dinosaur fossils that we have obtained have been found buried in the ground.

Fossils, or the preserved remains of animals, plants and other organisms from the remote past, prove that these amazing dinosaurs once roamed Earth. What would you do if you were in Mike's shoes and had to come face-to-face with living, breathing dinosaurs?

ABOUT THE AUTHOR

Bronx, New York–born writer and artist Franco Aureliani has been drawing comics since he could hold a crayon. Currently residing in upstate New York, USA with his wife, Ivette, and son, Nicolas, he spends most of his days in his Batcave-like studio where he works on comic projects. In 1995, Franco founded Blindwolf Studios, an independent art studio where he and fellow creators can create children's comics. Franco is the creator, artist and writer of Weirdsville, L'il Creeps and Eagle All Star, as well as the co-creator and writer of Patrick the Wolf Boy.

Franco recently finished work on Superman Family Adventures and Tiny Titans by DC Comics, and Itty Bitty Hellboy and Aw Yeah Comics by Dark Horse comics. When he's not writing and drawing, Franco teaches art.